A SILLY FLOP – FLIPPING PARADE

BY C. ROBERT BEALE

⊕ **Strategic Book Publishing**
New York, New York

Strategic Book Publishing
An imprint of Writers Literary & Publishing Services, Inc.
845 Third Avenue, 6th Floor – 6016
New York, NY 10022
http://www.strategicbookpublishing.com

ISBN: 978-1-60860-022-9   1-60860-022-X

Printed in the United States of America

Illustrations art, book cover art and book layout by
kalpart team - www.kalpart.com

To my son Christopher
for whom
this story was created.

O nce upon a time there was a man and his name was Flip. Everywhere Flip went he would do flips.

Flip, flip, flip.

Flip had a friend whose name was
Flop.
Everywhere Flop went he would do flops.

Flop, flop, flop.

Whenever they were together
people would see
Flip flipping and Flop flopping.

Flip-flop,

flip-flop,

flip-flop.

One day something terrible happened;
no one knows why but Flip started flopping
and Flop started flipping. Neither one could
stop or control where they were going.

Flop-flip,

flop-flip,

flop-flip.

They flopped and flipped out into the street and down the block, causing traffic to stop and people to stare.

No one could believe their eyes; it was such a shock to see them flop-flipping instead of flip-flopping.

When they came to the corner they met Carl the cop who was directing traffic.

"Help," they cried, "we can't stop."

When Carl the cop saw Flip flopping and
Flop flipping he was so surprised
that he nearly jumped right out of his shoes.
He began doing cartwheels.

It was unbelievable -- Flip was flopping,
Flop was flipping, and Carl the cop was doing
cartwheels.

Together the three men went down
the street. Car horns were honking and
little dogs were chasing them,
barking as loud as they could.
Everyone was looking to see what was
happening.

Seeing what was going on
had a strange effect on those
who were watching -- Hank the handyman
started doing handstands.

How could this be happening ...
Flip was flopping, Flop was flipping,
Carl the cop was doing cartwheels, and
Hank the handyman was doing handstands.

As the men went down Main Street
they passed the barber shop.
When Bob the barber saw them
he began bouncing a big beach ball.

Now there was Flip flopping, Flop flipping,
Carl the cop doing cartwheels,
Hank the handyman doing handstands,
and Bob the barber bouncing a big beach ball.

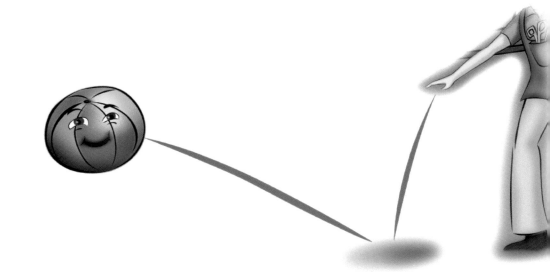

When Jim the junkman saw this
he started to juggle junk.
How absurd to juggle junk ...
but sure enough now there was Flip flopping,
Flop flipping, Carl the cop doing cartwheels,
Hank the handyman doing handstands,
Bob the barber bouncing a big beach ball, and
Jim the junkman juggling junk.

Steve the salesman came walking out of
a store just as they went by.
When he saw them he started
to sing silly songs.
Now there was Flip flopping, Flop flipping,
Carl the cop doing cartwheels,
Hank the handyman doing handstands,
Bob the barber bouncing a big beach ball,
Jim the junkman juggling junk, and
Steve the salesman
singing silly songs.

Things were really getting out of hand.
The traffic was snarled up and
drivers were getting angry.
Tim the truck driver got out of his truck
to see what the matter was.
Tim only added to the confusion
though by telling tall tales.

Now there was Flip flopping,
Flop flipping,
Carl the cop doing cartwheels,
Hank the handyman doing handstands,
Bob the barber bouncing a big beach ball,
Jim the junkman juggling junk,
Steve the salesman singing silly songs,
and Tim the truck driver
telling tall tales.

Finally, the whole strange parade came
to a little boy named Chris.
"Can you help us?" Called Flip and Flop.
"Sure," said Chris.
He reached out his hands and touched
them on the shoulders and
immediately they stopped.
They just stood there for a few minutes and
then went back to normal.

Flip went back to flipping. Flop went back to flopping. Carl the cop stopped doing cartwheels and went back to directing traffic. Hank the handyman went back to fixing things. Bob the barber gave Chris his beach ball and went back to cutting hair. Jim the junkman put the junk back on his wagon and went on his way. Steve the salesman went back to selling, and Tim the truck driver made his deliveries and then went home.

The whole town went back to normal, all because of a little boy who wasn't afraid to reach out and help someone in need.

THE END